Discovering my Omega

Werewolves of the West

Robert J. Morris

ISBN-13:9798695855944
ISBN-10:

Cover design by: Art Painter
Library of Congress Control Number: 2018675309
Printed in the United States of America

--Disclaimer--
This is a work of fiction. Names, places,characters and events are all ficticious for the reader's pleasure.Any similarities to real people, places, events, living or dead are all coincidental.

This book contains sexually explicit content that is intended for ADULTS ONLY. (18+)

*To my love john gardner for always telling me I
can do this and to never give up.*

Contents

1.Chance

My name is Chance Reynolds, I'm 25 years old. I was raised right here on my packs land my whole life and I remain here on this land even to this day. I love my days in the forest. This section of the Oregon national forest was amazing and full of everything a shifter could ever ask for. Endless acres for my wolf to run free and the respect of the neighboring packs.

Not long after my father the pack Alpha died; I was next to lead. Well every border Alpha thought it would be a good idea to take what was mine, so, I sent them home with more than just bruised egos. It also gave me the opportunity I needed to gain their respect while compelling my pack to fully accept me as their Alpha.

There was a new threat looming over me now though, and it wasn't money. We are a very wealthy pack, my grandfather saw to that. It was this idea I needed to have offspring to ensure my Alpha lineage would go on after I died. The pack had been quite patient with me because, they knew I was like many of the other males in the pack and preferred the company of men. It was our custom to be with whoever fate picked for us, and that's who we initiated the wolf bond with. So, there wasn't a female in the pack that was able to turn my head.

Then the strangest thing happened. I had just come in from my morning run when my second in command and best friend Jase, burst through my door.

"You **have** to come and see this, Chance, and not just because you're Alpha but because it's like a miracle for you and, he's gorgeous!" Jase said enthusiastically.

"Who is? What's going on?" I asked but got no answer.

Jase just grabbed my arm and pulled me to my large patio that overlooked the packs central gathering area. Normally nobody, and I mean nobody, was allowed to drag me anywhere. Being Alpha I had to keep everyone at an arm's length." Here they come. This wolf is a rogue, Chance. He's says he's alone and wants asylum." Jase stated.

I waited patiently until they stood at the foot of the patio. I started to speak when one of my pack guards snatched the strangers hood back. I almost tripped down on steps when I saw his face. Long brown shoulder length hair and a trim beard tan muscular body dusted with the perfect amount of chest and body hair. His tan skin shined in the morning sun from sweat and he looked exhausted from running from someone or something. But, as soon as our eyes met the wolf leapt in my chest and my canines started to grow out as my groin roiled with desire. I turned knowing I couldn't let my people see me like this, so, with my back turned I said,

" Take him into my living room. He and I have things to talk about and discuss. "I said in my best Alpha voice.

When they pulled and half dragged the man past me, I caught his scent and it was unlike anything I had ever smelled. Musk and pine with a touch of lavender. I had to find out who he was and who he was running from. My stomach was doing somersaults.

They sat the dirt covered man on the couch and he looked faint. I asked if he needed water and he nodded yes. I told the others," I am fine, leave the man here." and they reluctantly left. I got up went to the kitchen and got him a glass of cold water from the refrigerator and he gulped it down like he hadn't had anything to drink in days. "So, who are you running from?" I asked curiously.

He was shivering and looked up but wouldn't make eye contact. "My owners." he said." They want to –to—t- "and he fainted.

Great I thought, as I carried in the muscular, most attractive and dirty man I'd ever let into my bed. I waited for an hour but he was still out so I got up and told Hently to prepare us some roast beef sandwiches. Hently worked for my father and my grandfather so, he was old but, I couldn't make myself fire him so, he came to my house two days a week to make sure everything is in order. He does the household chores and occasionally cooks for me. About ten minutes later he brought the roast beef sandwiches in. Just as I was going to bite mine, I heard my guests heart kick up about ten paces and I knew then, he was awake even though he pretended not to be.

"You want this roast beef sandwich, and I uh, still don't know who you are. "I asked

"Anton." he mumbled.

" An- what?" I said loudly

"Anton", he said loud enough for me to hear.

"Oh Anton, ok, great name. Well do you? Want the sandwich I mean?"

"Please my Alpha?" he said quietly as he began to tremble. I reached out to him to steady him and he jerked away looking around wild eyed.

"Whoa, Anton, I wasn't going to hurt you, do you want this?" I asked as I held out the sandwich.

He gave me the strangest look, like he was studying my face but never my eyes, it was a little unnerving. He slowly reached for the sandwich like he could get beaten at any second and cautiously took it. He smiled a little and even gave a tiny snort as he began to inhale the sandwich. I took the plates and set them on the night stand, then got up and slowly made my way over to him from the reading chair in the corner of my bedroom. He stared at my feet as I walked towards him, shivering all the while.

I sat down on the bed beside him and instinctively stroked his hair, I couldn't help it, something screamed inside me to protect him and I had no idea why. It seemed to calm him and me strangely. I asked if he would like a bath? He looked me in the eyes for the first time and quickly nodded indicating a very enthusiastic yes. I was struck dumb by the beauty of those bright green eyes.

He stood up, but, got light headed. So, I grabbed him up in my arms and carried him to the bathroom, setting him on the toilet seat. I began to draw the bath and made it moderately warm, added the perfect amount of bubble bath then shut it off when it was full. I took off his shirt that was caked in mud and dirt and unbuttoned his pants and pulled them off. I almost lost my breath when I saw his markings. "OH, my god, he's, he's an Omega?" I thought to myself. I snapped back to reality and lifted him up carrying him into the warm water.

He stood on wobbly legs and I grabbed him and helped him sit and lay back in my large tub. He looked like he was in heaven. I was completely in shock; I mean an Omega? I had never seen an Omega; I had only heard of them in stories and old tales from years ago. This was real though; he WAS an Omega.

In the world of shape shifters Omega's are very rare and often hunted for sport because of their unique markings. They are the only males in any pack that can bear children. For any pack to have one is considered to be a great blessing from the heavens.

I paced in the living room for what must have been twenty minutes and completely forgot he was in there bathing until he sneezed and I ran in. Ok, we need to wash you. So, I soaped up a cloth and began to gently scrub under his arms and down his hard chest and rippled abs, down every extremity when I reached his manly bits. I just went about it, scrubbing partly with the cloth and then the rest with my soapy hand. Then he got a half grin and dunked under the water and came up all clean.

I didn't have the first clue what to do about him, but something was nagging me to take him in to nurse him back to health. No way was he going to the cells. I put him in my bath robe. We went into the living room because, my favorite show was coming on and I didn't want to miss it. Anton watched it with me for all of five minutes when he laid his head on my lap and said "Thank you Alpha." and fell sound asleep.

Later after my show, knowing he was exhausted from whatever he was running from, I scooped him up in my arms and laid him on my large king-sized bed and covered him up with the fluffy blanket. I returned to the living room and saw that Hently had left out some dinner, covered in a sliver plate cover. I uncovered the dish and gobbled down my dinner, tired from the excitement of the day.

I was driven by an indescribable force to go and lay with Anton, to feel his skin and smell his intoxicating scent. So, I crawled into the bed and made myself comfortable on my side and just stared at his brown auburn hair down his neck and his back all the way down to the blanket that stopped just above his waist. I shivered, I knew I felt different the closer I was to him, thrilled and even protective.

I awoke in the morning to the feel of his naked body against me. I smiled when I saw that he closed the distance between us in his sleep. His scent, oh god it drove me wild. I started to become aroused and the pressure in my groin grew. I began to back out of bed when he reached behind himself and grabbed at me, whimpering and pulling me back to him. Then I heard him whisper "Please Alpha?" and I caved in and put my arm around him. We both fell back to sleep.

2. Anton

I awoke to my new surroundings and for a moment I panicked, not knowing where I was, then it began to sink in, this odd sense of security. Then I realized my new Alpha was laying behind me pressed tightly against me with his hand gently resting on my hip. I sighed, and lay in silence but my Alpha said suddenly and softly "Do you want any breakfast?" I was thrilled and said, "Yes please, Alpha."

He leaned in quickly and gave me a peck on the cheek followed be a wide smile and put on his robe. Then he made his way to the kitchen and I could hear the sounds of the frying pans clanging. I got out of the soft heavenly bed, put my robe on and made my way to the kitchen bar to watch my new Alpha cook. I stood watching in amazement as he swiftly and precisely whirled about the kitchen cooking eggs toast bacon and pancakes. Oh, the sight of it all made my body tremble in anticipation of the feast being prepared before me.

After a short time, it was done and he gestured towards the dining room. I followed him and he sat my plate in front of the chair to his right. I sat and started out slow because of appearances. Then the reality of it being my first, real, meal in months kicked in. I began to scarf it down. My Alpha just smiled at me and said, "I'm glad you like it."

"It's wonderful I haven't eaten a real meal in—" I stopped myself. I didn't want to talk about what my family had done to me, why I ended up where I was being held so, I just finished with, "in days." My Alpha gave me a questioning look. I wasn't about to make eye contact so I went on to finish my last two bites and said "Thank you my Alpha." After he finished, he got up leaned over to grab my plate and I caught his scent, it was heady. It was the smell of leather and manly musk. I could swear he took a second to sniff me and then swiftly stood back up and cleared his throat, saying, "I'll get these cleaned up."

"Let me help you Alpha, you did cook, it's the least I c---" He broke in and said "YOU have to rest and take care of yourself so you can gain your strength back." With a beautiful wide smile.

I was surprised he cared but, I simply replied, "Yes Alpha."

I went and sat back at the kitchen bar and watched him clean up all the pans and dishes but, while I watched I was taken by his rugged handsomeness and chiseled features. He was very tall 6'4" maybe with broad shoulders. His square jaw was covered in a finely trimmed black beard and his wavey nicely cut hair shown auburn in the sunlight. His eyes sparkled golden brown in the light and my breathing increased as I caught myself staring. He had arms that could squash a bear and his scent was amazing. He was straight out of my every dirty fantasy.

I felt that familiar rush of heat flow through me and a chilling sensation crawl across my skin. "Oh, shit no, no not now!" I thought to myself. I was going into heat and the timing couldn't have been worse.

I rushed to the shower and picked out the smelliest body wash in their then hopped in. As I began lathering myself my mind drifted to his amazing smile and perfect body and I felt that hot rush again so, I turned the water to cold. I was hoping the smell of the body wash would help conceal my sexual pheromones because otherwise he would be able to smell my body's need to mate. The soothing cold water, I knew would only relax me temporarily. I rinsed off and shut the water off. Then stepped onto the soft fluffy mat to dry off. Then I found an old bottle of cologne and sprayed a bit on and hoped for the best.

By the time I made it to the living room he was sitting on the couch with a grin. "You feel better?" he asked still grinning.

"Yes, it was just what I needed." I said smiling back. I sat down next to him and he sniffed at the cologne I had on and smiled again. I was not sure what had him so giddy but I acted like I didn't notice.

Later that night I went to lay on the couch and he said, "No Omega, come lay in my bed, I won't bite."

"Yes Alpha." I replied as I made my way to his bed. I laid on what I considered to be my side and began shivering "Damn heat cycle." I thought to myself. I couldn't for the life of me get comfortable until he (out of either frustration or desire, I couldn't tell which) scooted up behind me, his firm body pressed tight against mine and put his hand on my hip. I was amazed at how much that soothed the ache inside me.

"How bad is it when you're in heat?" He asked softly. I felt like I was going to panic. I sat up and pleaded, "You know? Oh god don't, please don't, I'm not ready please!"

He quickly sat up and put a hand on each side of my face and said "Sh, sh, sh, I'm not going to do anything you don't ask me to do. Ok babe, just relax. Now lay back down and get some rest. Ok?"

"Shaking all over I cautiously said" Y-Yes Alpha." And laid back on my side "I know he's going to rape me, I know it" my fear crazed mind screamed. I laid there for an hour waiting for it but he had just leaned into my neck and took in a deep breath in of my scent and fell asleep. I was in shock none of the men who held me captive for so long would have been that kind. I sat up all night unable to sleep, my mind just whirling at the thought of being treated with such kindness.

Around sunrise Chance (as his inner circle calls him) began to stir and he slowly opened his eyes to see me gazing at him. I must have blushed because he said "Like what you see babe?" and then I noticed my erection was touching his stomach and I scooted back. "You don't have to be embarrassed, I liked it actually." He said as he smiled a sexy smile and hopped up out of bed.

I just laid there for a minute letting my erection slowly soften, then I got up and sat at the kitchen bar to watch him make breakfast. "So, do you eat like this every day?" I asked.

He said," I usually run in the mornings but you need the nourishment." And he smiled that sexy smile again.

This man is an Alpha and he's taking care of me? I wondered why, but didn't dare ask.

A while later we sat and had omelets and hash browns all cooked to perfection. After eating I helped him clean up and then he asked, "Will you go to town with me and help me with some shopping?"

"Of course, I said without hesitation. I hadn't been to a store in over six months and was thrilled at the idea.

"Great, get dressed and meet me out back behind the house." I quickly threw on my now clean clothes however torn and tattered and went out to the full-sized pickup truck under a parking shelter just out the back door.

As we made our way into town, I was fidgeting so he grabbed my hand and put it on his thigh with his large hand encompassing mine. I breathed in deep, just the touch of him made me feel calm and safe.

About fifteen minutes later we pulled up at the little mall and went into a pretty fancy men's clothing store. We went to the young men's section and started looking around. Then he pulled a shirt up against me as if measuring it against me then put it in the cart.

"What's happening here?" I asked genuinely curious.

"I'm getting you something to wear, you can't go around in those torn up clothes all the time." He replied and kept on shopping.

"But I can't pay you back, I have no money." I said with an air of concern.

"I don't mind and you need them so, let's shop, merry Christmas or happy birthday or whatever." He said with a smile.

I began to relax and get into it when he had me try everything on and I swear that took an hour solid. I had to come out and model each outfit. It was fun though and I hadn't had that kind of experience in my entire life.

We got to the counter and the nice lady rang everything up and I almost passed out when I saw the amount of 675.00$ come up on the display. I couldn't help but get excited and felt touched by the display of affection he showed when he grabbed all the bags and then grabbed my hand holding it tight.

When we got out into the parking lot, I caught a familiar scent and froze trembling. Chance could smell the fear I was putting off as he dropped the bags in the back seat and turned to me. "What's going on, what is it?" He said with a low growl, he knew something had me scared silent and he started scanning the area. Then they walked towards us laughing," Well, well look at the happy couple. You mind telling me what you're doing with my property?" Growled the man in the center of the trio.

"He's nobody's property so, who the hell are you and you'd be wise to tell me what you want before I get angry." Growled my new Alpha.

"We just want what's ours, so just hand him over before we kick your fucking ass stranger." The man said sternly

Chance just laughed and looked the man straight In the eyes as his claws and canines grew out. He took on the stance of a predator ready to attack when the three men backed away "You're a fucking Alpha? Fine have it your way but trust me when I say this isn't over!" then they turned and hurried off.

Chance just looked at me tenderly and grabbed me holding my trembling body. I couldn't muster the courage to tell him who the men were or what they had done to me. He just sighed and said "Just explain this to me when you feel ready babe." I felt a rush of relief as we climbed into the truck and drove back to his house.

I couldn't wait to put on my knew jammies that night so I showered and dried. Then I pulled up my silk Jamy bottoms and cashmere sweater and walked into the living room. He just smiled up at me and said perfect. Then he patted the cushion next to him and I sat down.

He threw his right arm around me and pulled me in close against him gesturing with the popcorn bowl he was willing to share, so I grabbed a hand full and munched on it savoring it. Everything I touched or ate lately felt like I was doing it for the first time. All I received in captivity were scraps or cold leftovers never more than once a day.

For the first time since my family sold me, I felt safe and cared for.

3. Chance

I still had yet to find out what had happened to my new Omega and the true question of whether or not he would be mine, was burning in my mind. I was new to the feel of this desire burning within me but, I could control myself and he didn't seem very receptive to the idea of mating anyways. I myself have never had sex with anyone, although I had fooled around with a few men. It never went as far as actual mating. I was just content to have someone around the house to fill the lonely hours.

I was getting sleepy and Anton had fallen asleep on my shoulder. I sat there for a while wondering what the hell had happened to him and who those men were but, I had no choice but to accept the fact he wasn't prepared to talk about it. I was not about to force him to tell me anything he didn't want to tell me.

I tried to wake him but he was still exhausted from his ordeal, so I carefully and gently lifted him up and carried him to bed. He mumbled the words, "thank you my Alpha." and smirked in his sleep. I thought it was adorable. I laid down in the bed next to him and he shimmied his way back against me and reached back grabbing my arm and wrapping it around him. So, I pressed in close to him and could smell his sweet scent heavy in the air and it was bliss.

When I got up just after dawn, he was not in the bed, he was gone. My first instinct was telling me he had run but, then the sounds coming from the kitchen told me otherwise. I sat up and stretched with a yawn then put my robe on and made my way to the kitchen to see what he was up to.

There he was, in his underwear with my apron on and a spatula in his hand. Omelets were cooking, stuffed with vegies and cheese and it smelled delicious.

"What are you up to handsome?" I asked as I flashed my best smile.

"Just cooking for my Alpha, I thought it was my turn to wait on you for a change. I've been here almost a week now and haven't cooked you anything." Anton replied with a sexy grin. I hadn't really seen him smile yet so, it was a singularly precious moment.

We sat down to eat and when I tasted that first bite I was immediately in heaven," This man can cook!" I thought.

After breakfast I asked if he would like to go for a walk, that is if he felt strong enough yet. He agreed with another gorgeous smile, this time a real smile. I was, needless to say, very happy to see him so alive for the first time since he arrived.

We walked the trail around the central part of the pack meeting grounds and stopped by a very old very massive pine tree surrounded by thick green grass. We decided to sit for a while and rest. I could sense his nervous energy and asked, "Are you ok babe, you seem upset about something?"

He just sighed and said, "It's time I tell you why I was running and who I was running from."

Then there was a long pause and I wasn't about to press him so, I patiently waited as I put my hand on his thigh and patted it consolingly." It's ok take your time babe."

He looked up at me and began to tear up, "I've never met anyone like you. you're kind to me. I don't want to keep anything from you, because it could put you in danger. My family never treated me kindly I've never really known kindness. I was sold almost three years ago in an arrangement with another pack. They wanted to make an alliance to go up against another pack they were at odds with. Well my owner locked me in a cage and Only came to see me when I---" Anton began to choke on the knot forming in his throat as he tried not to cry. The tears streaming down his face pulled at my heart strings, so I moved in and embraced him. He continued "When I was in heat. He would, you know, have his way with me in hopes I would give him an heir. Omega babies are a rare thing and that's what he was after."

Just then he broke down and sobbed for a moment, then gathered his composer and continued his horrific story, "About a month ago during my last cycle he left the cage door unlocked. As he cleaned up, I hit him with a rock and ran as fast as I could. They've been chasing me ever since."

Needless to say, I was at a loss for words. This all explains why he was so afraid for me to touch him and why the thought of sex frightened him so badly. He's never known tenderness or love. "I will protect you with my life and nobody is going to take you away ever again Anton. Even if you will not have me as your mate, I will see to it that you are always protected." I said as I pulled him to me in a tight loving embrace.

"Thank you, my Alpha, I would be so proud to be your Omega but I'm damaged goods. How could you not be disgusted to look at me?" He said with a look of such deep anguish.

I put my hand gently under his chin and brought his eyes up to meet mine. "I could never be anything but utterly and completely ecstatic to have you as my mate." I said in a gentle but stern tone.

He had no words to say, he just buried his face in my chest and cried while I rubbed his back and held him.

When he felt up to it, we decided to head back and have some lunch. We had been under that tree nearly three hours just lying in the shade holding hands. It truly was, wonderful.

We approached my house when Jase my second, ran up to me and said "Elder Olma has had a vision, she wants to see you and the Omega right away!" I held Anton's hand tight and we rushed to Olma's home next to the river. She was the only priestess in our pack and visions were only one of her many powers.

We stepped in to the doorway and she waved for us to enter. We approached as she pointed to her couch inviting us to sit.

"I have seen the yet to come and it concerns you and your Omega. But first you must understand that when an Alpha soul bonds with an Omega, a great power is unleashed within each of them. A power your inner wolfs will need in the months to come. Many trials and dangers will come to pass if there is to be true peace in your lives." She warned.

What is coming elder Olma? I don't understand." I pleaded in confusion.

"The future is not an unmovable stone but a dirt path, weaving this way and that, through the woods of the unknown. So, unlike the stone the dirt path can be created in the direction you choose. Do not fear young ones, it is within you to create a different path in life, or you can struggle to move the stone. The choice is yours."

As we left, I struggled to accept her words but Anton looked truly afraid. I tried to reassure him by stopping and turning him to face me, then I held his face in my hands and leaned in gently pressing my lips to his. When I stood up to look at him, he was smiling from ear to ear.

"What is it?" I asked truly clueless as to what had him smiling so wide.

"That was my first kiss." he said with a bashful look, still smiling.

I replied saying "I hope I did an ok job babe." Then I gave him a smile back and started heading back to the truck. I couldn't believe no one's ever kissed this gorgeous man. He just kept smiling and climbed into the cab as I shut the door for him.

We got home and he began to shiver. "Are you cold babe?" I asked concerned. "No, it's my cycle, the longer I'm alone the higher my fever gets and the worse the chills get. I just need to lay down for a bit and warm up."

"Ok, can I join you?" I asked truly trying to be sensitive now that I knew what he'd been through. He might not want me near him.

However, he grabbed my hand and smiled as he led me to the bed and took my shirt off. I did the same to him and we crawled under the covers. It didn't seem to help much until he asked me if I would hold him like I'd done the night before, when we were sleeping. I of course agreed and spooned up against his back and sure enough the touch of my skin calmed him and he stopped shaking.

After about thirty minutes I asked him if he'd be ok While I made dinner. He nodded yes and I crawled out and started cooking steak fillets on the grill. For sides I made baked potatoes with butter and pepper and asparagus. The smell of the meal cooking drew him out and he sat at the kitchen bar and watched me work.

After I made up our plates, I set them at the dining table, so we took a seat and started enjoying our meal together.

4. Anton

I couldn't help but laugh, he was so cute and so fun to be with. Every moment with him was something different and surprising, the good kind of surprising. I didn't know what I was feeling I just knew that all I wanted was to be with him and see that handsome smile.

He had my head whirling around the idea of actually being his Omega and what that would be like. I quickly pushed those thoughts aside and concentrated on what he was saying. I laughed as we went into the living room to watch some TV when the news came on "Special report; the father of Anton Winters has come forward to the media claiming their brother has been kidnapped and is being held against his will by this man shown here in this store security camera footage. They are suspected to be camped out in the Willamette national forest.

My Alpha knew the local sheriff's department and cleared everything up as long as I would turn in a hand written affidavit.

I almost screamed but I started to panic and I couldn't catch my breath. I started to feel light headed when my Alpha must have seen the look on my face, because he grabbed me and held me tight against him whispering words of comfort. I started to think about what it would feel like to be locked up again, if they take me again and my legs felt weak. I felt them give then I felt my Alpha cradling me in his massive arms. He carried me to the bedroom and took off my shirt and slid down my pants then he lifted my legs up and under the covers and then tucked me in. I watched half aware of what was happening as he took his clothes off and crawled in next to me wearing nothing but his boxer briefs. I felt his warm soft skin and hard muscles flex as he positioned behind me and wrapped his arm around me until I stopped shaking. Then he whispered "Nobody in the world can ever take you from me baby, I will take on the world and win to protect you."

Those words he whispered hung with me the rest of the night. I couldn't seem to get to sleep so, I just laid there wrapped in his comforting embrace. I knew they would never stop looking for me, he couldn't be there all the time, one day they WILL take me from him and I would be helpless to stop them. I suddenly got so angry I had to get up so I slowly scooted out from under his arm and went into the living room. I paced back and forth talking to myself reminding myself how weak and pathetic I was. How I was good for nothing more than a tool to make babies I would never be allowed to hold. I started sobbing into my hands when I felt him wrap his arms around me "Sh,sh,sh, you are safe, you are beautiful and you are the most important person in my life." He said as he pulled my chin up to look me in the eyes, I could barely see his handsome smile through the blur of my tears. It made me smile though. "Never forget who you are ok. You are Anton and you're beautiful, sexy and strong. I want you to tell yourself that everyday baby." He said then pulled me into the bathroom for a relaxing shower. I felt like a king for the first time in my life, I felt important. He took the wash cloth and gently rubbed every inch of me with it never breaking eye contact, it was heaven.

Then he took the shower wand and rinsed every inch of me. Then shut off the water. I tried so hard not to look but I had to peek so, I looked down and was amazed at how massive and delicious his dick looked. I know I got caught because when I looked up, he was just smiling as he dried me off. After he dried himself off it was about sunrise so he said he was going for his run before breakfast. I wanted so badly to object but I couldn't, not after all he'd done for me.

So, I nodded and went back into the bedroom to lay back down. A few minutes later I heard the door open, then close and then the click of the lock. I knew I was safe but a voice just kept screaming at me to run. I shook my head and reminded myself how he'd driven them off at the mall. I think mostly out of exhaustion from not sleeping much I fell asleep and the next thing I knew I could smell waffles and strawberries in the air. I got out of bed and my Alpha said "There you are babe, I'm glad you're up here's some breakfast." And he sat a huge plate of waffles and strawberries with whipped cream in front of me. I couldn't help but just dig in.

After breakfast we went for a walk and ended up under the same tree as before, so we laid down right there in the shade and talked. "I want to try." I said," I want to be yours and only yours, if you will have me still." I was so ashamed and terrified he would reject me, I looked away. He pulled my chin to face him and he had the biggest smile I'd ever seen as he said, "I've never been so happy as I have been these last two weeks. I think you were made for me and I for you because you bring out the true Alpha in me. I'm falling in love with you baby." Then he leaned in and kissed me long and gentle. I heard a longing growl in his chest and it made me feel so special.

We made our way back to the house and went in to get out of the sun. I made it as far as the living room when I felt an arm grab mine and gently turn me to face him then he kissed me this time passionately and deep as he held me in his strong arms. I knew that I wasn't in heat anymore so this was him just wanting me for me. I wanted to know his heart and desires. He laid me back on the couch and sat down on the floor next to me and began threading through my hair with his fingers, it felt so good. To say I was relaxed was an understatement.

The next day he got so excited I didn't see him the first half of the morning then when he got back, he told me he wanted our bonding to be honored by the pack. And blessed by Olma the pack priestess. I had no problem with any of it so I said, "Great that's nice." then he said, "What are we going to wear at the party." I wanted to just crawl in a hole I said, "OH, people really, not just you and me huh?" He turned and laughed at me saying, "What? No way, the pack will be there silly and Olma."

"Oh, ok, I'll wear that nice suite you got for me at Armani's." I said in defeat.

"Great baby, I can't wait to be announced with you next to me." He said grinning so wide and proud It made it worth a little anxiety.

I got ready to be out the door by six thirty. Chase arrived on the front patio right on time and came in and just stopped while he stared at me. "What's wrong with me, what?" I asked anxiously but he just smiled wide and said, "You're perfect."

I honestly never felt so confident in my life. "I can do this shit no problem. My Alpha says I'm perfect, so I'm doing something right."   I thought to myself as we climbed into the truck. When we arrived one of the packs kids a young man in his teens was playing valet so he took the truck and we went in. There was music and dancing and wine, oh thank god there was wine. Needless to say, I hit the bar running. Then after my third glass I went and grabbed My Alphas hand and held it tight while he made small talk with one of the elders in the pack. Then we made the customary round about the place. Everyone was very kind and respectful they almost treated us like royalty. I was not used to being treated humanely much less treated like I'm special. Then, like he could read my mind, he leaned into me and said" You are the best thing to ever happen to me. You're the most special person I've ever met baby." Then kissed me on the cheek.

The night had gone by smoothly but I still insisted on keeping my buzz up. Then it was time for the blessing. We fastened our jackets and made our way to the center of the stage where Olma stood. She was wearing a beautiful beaded dress. She reached out to us as she took my right hand and his right hand and put them together. Then she wrapped our hands in a white silk ribbon and began a beautiful chant spoken in the old language of their ancestors. After she finished the amazing chant she leaned in and said, "I am happy you have chosen to make your own path through the woods." And she smiled as they helped her off stage. My Alpha and I still tied together received a standing ovation as we walked down off the stage. I just smiled and waved and he did the same. Then we headed out front where the truck was parked running and waiting for us. I climbed in and Chance shut the door for me then he drove me home and smiled the whole way.

5. The Longest Wait

It was customary for the bonding couple to actually bond after they got home from the party but he didn't want our first time together to feel pressured or for me to feel obligated. So, he just held me tight against him and I buried my face in his chest hair and he kissed my forehead as we fell asleep in each other's arms.

The next week and a half flew by, as we learned everything, we could about one another. Then the inevitable happened and he had to leave for three days to the city to discuss a land proposition he'd been working on. The deal was to procure more land from the government under his license as a nature conservation specialist-Alpha.

It was day three and I was feeling very fidgety and nervous everything was pissing me off, even the damn birds that I usually love. I knew something was up but I couldn't put my finger on it. Then later that day I felt it. The heat ran up my spine and into my chest and I began to sweat. Then I felt the chill crawl over my skin and I knew, I was going into heat again. I needed sex to calm my raging hormones but I was still afraid. Besides I did it last month I can do it again.

Then Chase my Alpha came through the door and scared the shit out of me. I smiled wide and hugged him. He leaned into me and said, "Oh god baby you make me crazy when you smell like this." I felt him shiver with the feeling of want and desire like I felt. But I wasn't sure if I could yet.

We had a wonderful dinner of lobster and fillet mignon. Fruit and cheeses from all over the world. He had grabbed take out from our favorite seafood restaurant in town. We finished up and went to the couch to watch some TV. I tried to sit away so I didn't drive him crazy with my pheromones but he wanted me close so I laid up against him and rested my head on his shoulder.

It was about one thirty and we were tired now so we decided to go to sleep. We crawled into bed and he scooted up against me and as soon as he took a breath, I could feel his growing arousal on my bottom. I thought. "This sweet man was just going to let me torture him as long as I needed to and he would never force me to do anything or force himself on me, I was genuinely safe."

That was the clencher and I knew tonight was the night. So, I crawled out of bed and turned to face the man that was grunting in protest. I started taking off my bed clothes and he just lay there watching his mouth half open. I was crazed inside. I never realized until this moment just how much I craved to be wrapped in those arms while he made love to me. I had butterflies in my stomach just thinking about being made love to.

I slowly pulled down my briefs and he licked his lips at the sight of my hard response to the situation. I yanked the covers off of him and crept across the bed. His countenance gave way to a huge animated smile. That eased my nerves a little. I laid down next to him and guided his hand to my erection. He rubbed it gently then began to stroke it in smooth and even strokes. I closed my eyes and leaned back, then I felt the bed shift and the most wonderful sensation ravaged me. I looked down in amazement to see his mouth fully engulfing my cock with a smooth pace. I have never felt that before and I reveled in it. Then he abruptly sat up, pulled his underwear off and laid down beside me, looking into my soul. He began to move towards me like a cautious predator and I remained resolute. I heard him growl a guttural rumble as he hovered over me and took in my scent.

Then he softly said, "I don't know what to do baby, I'm sorry." His eyes shied away and I pulled his chin so he faced me and I smiled saying, "First time for us both, we got this." Then I rolled over onto my tummy and stuck out my ass instinctively. He answered with curiosity as he smelled the air and followed the scent to my tight opening. He began to lick at my hole then my wetness came and he growled louder as he lapped it up with his tongue.

Suddenly like instinct took over he knew just what to do. He positioned over me and I could feel his cock spread my cheeks but, he stopped and leaned down to my ear asking sincerely, "Do you want this Anton, my Omega?"

"Oh god yes, please Chance, my Alpha!" I groaned. He stood to his knees and pulled my ass up to meet his cock. Then he pushed and my own erection jumped and began to leak with anticipation. He gently pushed and my back arched as he entered me. The sensation was different than any other time in my young life. This was the result of love. This intense feeling of pleasure and excitement overpowered me. He began to thrust deep into me softly pressing my sweet spots inside, rubbing against every wild nerve within me and I groaned in ecstasy. It was amazing and so different.

My body was his wholly. I was his. His massive member filled my wanting canal and I moaned again. My moisture came out of me as he thrust. He stopped and bombarded my hungry wet hole with his tongue and I could hear the intensity of his passion grow by the sound of the low rumble coming from deep in his chest. He was driven now by the taste of me, so again he stood to his knees and slowly and gently filled me again. I writhed in pleasure as he pumped in and out, making me feel complete and beautiful. I felt the sensation of being wanted jolt through me and it made every touch and every intimate moment that much more intense.

His thrusts came quicker now and I felt his strength and his passion with every movement. I could feel his sweat dripping onto my back and it spurred me on. I grabbed my own cock and began to work it fast and smooth. Then he pulled my hand away and began to work my cock with his hand, in motion with his every thrust. All the sensations filling me inside and out now had me breathing ragged breaths of pleasure. He was close I could tell and so was I. I felt his Knott begin to swell, lighting up every sensitive nerve inside me. He started to shutter as his orgasm grew closer. He kissed my neck then he bit down with his canines and growled as our souls intertwined in a magical bond to form one. I was his and he was mine forever now. Then he spilled inside me. My own cock was unable to hold back the flood that followed. We collapsed together on the bed. We were knotted so, he pulled me up to him and spooned me as we each fought to catch our breath. When his breathing was less ragged, he softly said "Did I do an ok job, my Omega?"

I giggled and said "You were amazing my Alpha; I've never felt so loved in my life." He wrapped his arm around me and held me tight against him as we softly drifted off together.

The middle of the night got cold and I woke up freezing so, I unwrapped myself from my Alpha and felt the strange sensation of him fall out of me. We had been knotted for quite some time, it being his first time and all. I then gathered the sheet and blankets and threw them over Chance and the bed. I crawled under the covers and he pulled me to him as he softly snored.

The next morning, he was full of life and energy. He smiled down at my sleepy face and kissed my forehead, then hurried out the door for his morning run. I managed a shower to wash the sex off myself and put on my bath robe before he returned. He jogged in and stopped, breathing heavy, his chest hair curled against his moist muscled flesh. The sight of the broad sexy sweaty hunk of an Alpha in front of me had me getting wet again. I could feel my body respond and I dropped my robe to the floor and laughed as I ran into the bedroom. By the time he made it in he was completely undressed and hard as stone, throbbing with every beat of his heart.

I put out my arms and he got a huge smile and growled playfully at me as he laid on top of me gently. I knew what I wanted and it was him, inside me, now. I pulled my legs up towards my chest and reached down to gently guide his swollen member. When I had him positioned, I softly said," Now baby, push inside."

My body spasmed as his massive cock entered me. He sniffed and kissed my neck feverishly. I held his hard-tight ass as he thrust into me. He grunted and pushed faster and faster both our bodies wanting what the other had to give. My wet canal was wrapped tightly around his manhood. I pulled and scratched at his ass and he growled in pleasure as it drove his climax further to the surface. He began to swell and I knew it would be soon, soon I would have his essence in me again. He curled into me and spilled inside me in pleasure.

He collapsed onto me and we both laughed at each other over our insatiable need for one another. He rolled to my side spooning me until his Knott went down and we could get up.

The animal within me calmed as the sexual burn in my skin subsided and I knew that the insanely incredible sex we had, satiated my inner beast. I knew I would have relief from my cycle for good because, he was powerful and it seemed he could stave off my heat cycle. I got back in the shower only this time Chance joined me. We loved the feel of one another so, we always seemed to wash each other. After we were clean again, we stepped out of the massive walk in shower and dried off.

6. The obvious conclusion

It had been just over two months since Chance and I had mated for the first time. To be honest it was like I had never done it before, because my first time with chance was so incredible. But that thought was not the primary thought that was on my mind. I hadn't had a cycle in nearly a month and a half. I was so scared because we had never talked about having babies and it was so soon after life-bonding with him. I just didn't know how to tell him.

Chance walked in and of course he had a shitty day but he could smell my fear in the air. He turned to me with concern and said, "Omega, baby, are you alright?"

I started to pull away from him and he gripped me firmly and pressed, "Baby, what's wrong, please tell me?"

I was at a loss so I started to cry and just blurted, "I'm pregnant Alpha!" and backed away. He had the oddest expression so I just stood there. Then a huge smile took over his features and he jumped and hollered, "WE'RE HAVING A BABY! He began to jump up and down until his breath gave out, then he swept me up in his massive arms as he said, "Anton, my Omega, why were you afraid? I would never be mean to you, you know that."

I replied "I know my Alpha, I just get stuck in the past sometimes I really am trying to put it behind me though, I swear."

He responded with "Baby it's a part of who you are and as awful as it was, it is part of why you're a wonderful person. I love you my Omega" and he gave me a tight squeeze.

"What do we do baby? I mean you need to see a doctor right. How long has it been do you think?" He asked in concern.

"About eight weeks since I was supposed to cycle." I replied scowling.

He stood up and said well I'll call the pack OB and get you in tomorrow.

So, we ate and giggled again about having a baby. It was an amazing feeling seeing him so excited and it was something I was able to do for us, for him. I felt like I was beaming.

The next morning, we got up got dressed and went to see the doctor. We were so excited and overjoyed we could barely contain it. We calmed a bit when they called out "Anton Winters?" We hopped up and went in smiling wide. Her name was Dr. Lena Simms. The first thing she did was run the blood before anything else, so it could come back before we left. She began the pelvic exam. I stood bent over a table while she probed up my rear and into my birth canal. It hurt like hell but she was done quick enough. "Everything looks fine but I am required by law to ask any Omega that walks in these doors this question if I see the signs. Who raped you son?" She asked very tenderly. I just shuffled in my seat and said "I, I, Well I've never been."

"Yes, yes you have dear but if you're frightened that the son of a bitch who did this is going to come after you, he won't because he will be in jail." She said with conviction but I just shook my head. She handed Chance her card and said" If he's ever ready, just call us.

Then she got a listen to my tiny flat six pack I felt so ridiculous. But she said" Yep only one." I let out a huge sigh of relief because twins were a big thing in my family. Then she got the bloodwork back and she told us to sit. My heart jumped and I felt panic set in but I stayed focused on what she was saying. After a moment She looked up and said "You have what's called in the case of Omegas a High potential for toxoplasmosis in other words your kidneys may not be able to handle a baby right now. You are very young since at twenty-one you've had cycles for less than a year now. It is in my strong opinion that you need to terminate and try again in two or three years. I see this a lot in Omegas that are too young to be having babies."

I was in shock, I'd never been happier than I was this morning, now she was telling me no I couldn't have this baby! Well I've been controlled my whole life and I will not allow it ever again! "I'm sorry doctor but I'm having this baby. If it kills me so be it but, I will do something with my life other than just survive. I want to have my life mean something!" I just turned and left. Chance stayed with the doctor a few more minutes and then we headed for the car." Please Baby, think about what you're doing. God damn it, I can't lose you, please don't do this." He said as his voice cracked from holding back a sob.

I didn't know what to say so I just grabbed his hand and kissed it then held it in my lap. We drove in deafening silence, Chance either couldn't or wouldn't speak to me. When we got home, I asked him if he wanted lunch and he just replied "I'm going for a run, I'll be back later." I tried to say be careful but he was gone.

I was scared but I wasn't going to just give up either, if I was like that, I would have died a teen. About two hours later he came in the door sweaty and looking exhausted. He just turned down the hall and went into the bathroom to take a shower.

We had been together for months now, I'd never seen him mad at me or cry and today he had been privy both. I was off my game, to say the least I had no idea what I was doing.

He came out after his shower and hugged me tight then he pushed his face into my shoulder and sobbed. He cried so hard that we dropped to our knees while I tried to comfort him. My Alpha, my big strong man could cry? I suddenly felt so guilty. I'd never even taken the time to think about how he would feel. I just sat there and held him while he calmed down and he looked up and said "I can't lose you baby, my sweet Omega." And softly stroked my face with the back of his hand.

I reassured him it was only a chance that the worst could happen. I tried to convince him how strong I was, but he interrupted with a serious look on his tear stained face. "OK, this is how this is going to happen. You see the doctor once a month nonnegotiable and the nurse comes by once a week to draw blood and take measurements. You will have to change your diet and you won't like it, also you need to take these supplements every day. Are we cool?"

"Cool as ice my Alpha." Then I smiled and whispered "I love you."

He managed a smile and said "You are my forever, without you There will be nothing for me in life." And we held one another.

The next days went by fast and so did the two weeks after that. He began to accept my decision and began to buy baby equipment and baby proofing stuff and a baby crib.

"A crib? Isn't it a little early?" I asked with a smile. He replied saying, "OH, I think not. You stormed out while I got told what was going to happen if you did this. You my dear Omega are going to start showing and I mean fast." Then he got a shit eating grin that just really twisted my tit. I said "OH, is that so and how does someone who has six months left to go start to show? Hmm answer me that my Alpha."

He kept on smiling and I knew I was in for some shit. "Well let's see, you're not human you're an Omega and that leaves you with twelve to sixteen weeks to go not sure exactly." He said still grinning. "Oh, hells bells. "I thought to myself. He knows more about this than I do. I had to start studying this and fast.

7. Coming to terms

"I sure hope he starts thinking about what he's doing here." I thought to myself. I knew I wouldn't be able to stand my life without him in it. I didn't like the fact he was taking such a huge risk but, I tried to be understanding and help him through this. I loved him so much that it ached and I knew I would love our baby too. I walked into the room and caught him looking at his tummy in the mirror and I said teasingly" "Nope, still a six-pack babe."

I don't know if he appreciated my humor or not but, I thought it was funny. Then over the next three weeks just like the doctor said he just started showing and it seemed to happen overnight. His six pack was getting less defined and he had a little tummy sticking out just a bit. I took it upon myself to start kissing his tummy and not his lips, but that only lasted a few days, then I couldn't take it anymore. I had the crib done, and started on the arduous task of redecorating the room.

So far, everything was looking normal with the baby and Anton, so that settled my nerves a bit. I didn't know what the future had in store for us but I knew we would face it together. The longer we were together the more he called me by my given name and not by my title. I liked it much more than I thought I would. It was very personal and That's what made it all the more special.

"Chance baby?" He asked with a hint of timidness in his voice.

"Yeah babe. What's the matter?" I replied.

"I need to go to the store and get my prescriptions, can you take me, I don't want to drive?" He said

"Of course, baby why would you be worried about asking me for anything? I thought we were past this?" I said in a gentle tone.

"I know, I am, I just didn't want to interrupt you since you're busy." He replied with a smile.

"I'm never too busy to take care of my sweet Omega." I said kissing him and his tummy.

We piled into the truck and headed into town. It was a semi small town but it had anything one needed at least. We got to the pharmacy and I went in for him and got the prescriptions. On my way out I dropped the bag when I saw his truck door opened and he was missing.

"BABY? Where are you? ANTON?" I screamed but I heard nothing. I started to move around the parking lot.

"Anton baby, where are you?" I yelled, then I heard a muffled sound and ran in its direction. The wolf in me starting to emerge and my fangs and claws came out, my eyes took on their usual yellow glow and my heightened senses took over. I caught my Omega's scent and followed it. I heard him scream my name and I ran as hard as my wolf could move. I heard the engine start and I turned in its direction. I reached for the trunk as the tires screeched and the car took off at full speed. A huge plume of smoke billowed as they started to pull away from me. I ran with everything in me I ran but, I wasn't fast enough. I was the fucking Alpha of 110 werewolf's and I couldn't catch a fucking car.

I ran back to the truck as fast as my arms and legs could take me and jumped in. I started the truck and drove as quickly as possible to the packs meeting grounds and howled for my inner circle. They ran up to me, transformed back into human form and knew by the look on my face that something was very wrong.

"They took him they took my Omega!" I said with a growl.

"Who did Alpha?" Jase asked in concern. Jase liked Anton and if I knew my second, he would stop at nothing to get my Omega back.

"We need a plan how are we even going to find them or who they even are." Jase asked his brow furled.

"We need to hit up our contacts in the underground and tell them we are looking for a pregnant Omega for sale. It's the only thing I can think to do that will draw them out." I stated, still in shock.

We gathered all the inner circle and informed them of the plan and who would be doing what exactly. Then we waited. Time seemed to slow to a crawl every hour was anguish. It hurt me in my chest and sometimes I couldn't breathe. I couldn't allow myself to think the worst. I had to believe it was the men I had confronted us in the parking lot not long after meeting Anton, my Omega. That way, there was a very likely chance that they wanted to sell him or sell the baby. It had been two days now and I was in ruin. I sat in the middle of the living room floor drinking whiskey and thinking about the day I told him I wanted to bond with him. His beautiful face and the wonderful feel of his touch. I had begun to think the worst. I sobbed and then I heard a knock from the door.

"Fuck off please!" I yelled through the door. Then I heard Jase.

"We got a lead Alpha!" I ran to the door wiping my face off and opened the door saying," What, where, where is he?"

"We don't know but, someone called Samuel wanted to put out a price on a pregnant Omega. It sounds like our people Chance." Jase explained.

"Get the boys ready and set up the buy we do this tonight or tell them no sale and go high on the opening offer so they bite." I'm gonna shower while you and the boys work out the details ok." I said.

"Sure Chance, and hey man, Brush your damn teeth you smell like booze." Jase said teasingly and smiled as he backed away.

I gave him a grateful look because, I needed something to lift my spirits and finally, I had hope again.

Drew, (one of my inner circle of werewolf guards) Called Samuel and made the offer so, we waited for the call back. I fidgeted and the boys could no doubt smell my fear but, they could tell the difference between fear and concern so I didn't let it bother me. Five minutes then ten and I was getting anxious again. Then the phone rang and Drew put Samuel on speaker. "I got you buddy, they bit and you need to be at Smithwyk park by ten tonight with the hundred grand, ok?"

"Sure thing Samuel, thanks you're a real pal." Drew said.

"Ass kiss." Samuel said and hung up.

It was nine forty so we had to hurry. The boys and I piled in the van and took the forest service roads to the edge of the pack's boundaries. Jase took his red pickup and headed for the meeting spot. The boys and I arrived about fifteen minutes later because it was a hell of a lot shorter through the woods. All the boys spread out into position and I came to the center nearest to the exchange location.

About ten on the dot they pulled up and got out. There were six of them carrying automatic weapons. The man from the parking lot was in the center.

Jase got out with his hands in the air and walked closer to the man in the center, then showed him the money. The man examined the cash and Jase demanded to inspect the Omega first. The guy just chuckled. Then it happened, my baby stepped out of the back of the car, his hands were bound and he was muzzled. My wolf started to rage and claw inside me and I desperately wanted to let him out to rip these fuckers to pieces But, I stayed the course. Then the man took the money and shoved my baby to the ground at Jases feet.

That was all I could handle I started to transform as my throat howled loud in the light of the crescent moon and I leapt from the shadows sliding to a stop between the men and the car, blocking their escape. They pointed the guns and started shooting as I leapt up onto the car, then onto one of them, biting down on his skull with a cracking sound. I turned my attention to the man trying to reload the rifle and lunged, sliding as I slashed with my razor like claws and his innards fell to the ground with a plopping, sloppy sound. I then turned to the man, the one, the fucker who took my Omega, my sweet Omega. My brain boiled with rage. I leapt as a shot rang out, I chomped down on his throat, taking his esophagus with me.

I spat the man's throat out and transformed to my human form and ran to my Omega, who was being shielded by Jase. Jase backed up as I approached.

"Oh god Anton baby, are you hurt? Is the baby ok?" I asked desperately needing to hear the words, yes, we're fine.

"I'm ok Chance But, I don't know about the baby. I think something is wrong." He said with a look of terror on his face that made me feel sick to my stomach.

"Ok baby, you're going to be fine. Let's go Jase we need to get to the hospital now!" I said as Jase swiftly jumped behind the wheel.

After Anton got in and settled, we sped out of the park and made our way to the hospital. I cleaned myself up on the way. I carried Anton through the doors and yelled, "Help, please someone, he needs help! Our baby please!"

A nurse and one of the emergency room doctors came running up to us and said "ok sir, please we need you calm to support dad here, ok?

I forced myself to be cool and be more the Alpha I knew he needed. So, I relaxed the best I could and held my Omega's hand. A doctor came in and said, "Hello my names doctor Philips and I'm going to run some tests and see what's happening inside, ok?"

We just nodded struck dumb by everything that has happened and we watched as she pulled up Anton's shirt and pressed the ultra sound against his tummy. She said, "There we go, don't be alarmed but, there is a tiny bit of tearing on the canal wall. This can happen if you have a bad fall or get into an accident. It's not life threatening to you or the baby but, you need to take it easy and let this heal naturally, ok?" She stated in a very calm, professional yet compassionate voice.

I looked at Anton as he looked at me and we embraced as he cried. The doctor stepped out and Anton held my face in his hands and said, "My man, my Alpha, you came for me, you saved me." Then he burst into tears again as I held him tight.

"I will always save you my Omega, always no matter what, I will always be there for you baby." I said sincerely because, never again would anyone take my love from me. I will walk through hell to protect my little family with all my strength.

Just then I went to stand up and slipped on something. I could smell the strong metallic odor of blood. I looked down and blood trailed down my side and was running down my leg onto the floor and not slowly either. I unzipped my coat and said "Oh hell!" then my head felt fuzzy and things started to feel strange. "Oh shit, I'm passing out babe but, don't panic we're in a hospit---" I fell to the floor with a massive crash as I took a tray of exam equipment down with me.

8. Anton

I wanted to be the first thing that Chance saw when he woke up. I was asleep in the hospital recliner next to Chance's bed. I must have dozed off because when I woke up, he was just staring into my eyes like he did when we first met.

"Hey babe, you feeling better?" I asked with concern written all over my face.

He just looked up at me and smiled. "You're high on the pain med's, aren't you?" I asked. He nodded and smiled again.

"I love you with all my heart Chance, my Alpha." I said as I choked back my tears. I hated seeing my strong man wounded and defenseless. It broke my heart. I called the nurse and let her know that he was awake. "Thank you I'll let the doctor know." She said then she hurried out.

After about twenty minutes the doctor popped in and with a loud voice and said "Mr. Reynolds, how are you feeling?"

"I feel pretty good, actually I'm sure I'm healing very fast." Replied Chance.

" Well that's exactly what I was thinking, unless you wish to stay, I've written up your discharge papers." Now in regards to the wound, I want you to keep it clean and do not get it wet for twenty-four hours. You should be healed by then. The bullet went clean through missing your organs and kidney. You're a very lucky man. Your mate already spoke to the police but, they still want a statement so, here's their card. Well just follow the discharge instructions and you should feel fine in a couple days. Call us if anything changes." He said and then walked out with a half-smile.

About ten minutes later the nurse brought in Chance's pants, they had been washed and his shirt was stained but, clean but, had the bullet hole in it. I helped him dress and called the nurse. She went over the home care instructions and sent us on our way. By the time we got to the exit Jase was waiting for us, so we helped Chance into the truck and we were on our way home.

Once we arrived at the house, I helped him to the bedroom and undressed him and he laid back with a grunt. I went in a few minutes later to check on him and he was asleep. He had a huge erection so, I thought what would my Alpha do? So, I gently crawled up onto the bed and

Careful not to rouse him, then I slowly tugged on his briefs and pulled them down just far enough. Then I took his massive cock into my wanting mouth and began to suck and bob in waves of desire. I savored the taste of him and he began to moan and gently push up into my mouth.

His right hand clenched the bed sheets and the other threaded through my hair as his desire increased to ecstasy and he began to leak. I could taste his arousal on his manhood and it made the animal within me go wild. I longed to have his essence in my mouth so I worked him faster twisting and turning my head teasing the head of his massive member with my tongue. I took it deep to the back of my throat and beyond, he was crawling with exhilaration as his climax shuddered within him, screaming to be set free. Unable to refute it any longer he gently spasmed and groaned as he filled my mouth with his seed. I moaned and savored every drop as he became still and smiled down at me.

I threw myself into his waiting mouth and we kissed deep and passionately. I backed away and smiled down at him and said, "Bet you didn't see that one coming huh?" He started to laugh as he grabbed his side, trying not to cause himself anymore pain.

Later that afternoon He came walking out of the bedroom as I was making dinner and sat at the kitchen bar. I turned around and saw him and asked "Are you healed enough to be out of bed babe."

"Yeah baby I'm healing fast. By tomorrow I'll be right as rain and back to me old self again." He said with a smile.

"Good I've missed you during TV time and of course every other time too." I stated with a grin.

He just smiled winked at me and made his way to the couch. I put out some tv trays and then served chicken marsala with steamed broccoli.

I'm guessing he liked it because it was gone faster than I've ever seen him eat, and I was the pregnant one. His body needed the nutrition because he was healing so fast. I went ahead and made the fried ice cream I had already prepped in the freezer.

It was around ten and we decided to call it a night, he was tired from his body healing and I was just tired from all the stress of the last week. We made our way into bed and he snuggled up behind me and we fell fast asleep.

The next morning, I woke up to the familiar sound of pans and the wonderful aroma of bacon. I put on my robe and went out and sat at the kitchen bar like I always did in the mornings. He smiled at me and leaned over the counter giving me a kiss on the cheek. Oh, I was back in heaven, safe with my big strong Alpha.

The pain I had in the side of my abdomen had subsided and I knew the tearing on my canal wall had healed. We spent the day cuddling on the couch then he had a pack meeting to head to and I took the opportunity to take a much-needed nap.

After Chance returned home from the meeting, he woke me when dinner was ready and I slowly staggered my way to the dining room with a yawn.

After dinner was over, we sat to watch TV when someone knocked on the door. Chance got up and went to see who it was. He came back with a look of confusion on his face.

"That was Chance, Elder Olma needs to see us right away; she's had another vision." Chance said with an er of concern.

I got my street clothes on and we headed over to her cabin on the lake. We were about to knock when the door opened and she stood there gesturing us to sit on the couch. We did as she wished and made ourselves comfortable.

"Ah, young ones. I see you are blessed with new life." She said with a smile.

"Yes, elder Olma, we are having a baby soon." I replied.

"All the better I tell you what my vision has shown me." She stated.

"I saw flames and smoke rising in the night sky and our people were fighting a great evil. Evil that shined like black mountain glass and flame. I saw the specter of death seeking its prey. The clapping of thunder and the ground was bright with blood. Then the blackness covered the forest in darkness." Olma said in a very concerned tone. She continued saying," Be vigilant and mind the shadows young ones. Do not trust your eyes for they cannot see through the darkness lurking.

Then she looked at my tummy and smiled then showed us to the door.

"Elder Olma, what does it all mean?" Chance asked in confusion.

"It means nothing if we are strong and stay true to one another." She replied.

We drove home in silence pondering the words she spoke and the cryptic yet dreadful possibilities of them.

In the following weeks her words seemed to weigh less heavily on us. We resumed our walks on our favorite trail and my tummy had grown considerably. We rested under our tree. Chance leaned back against its great trunk and I laid on my back resting my head on Chance's leg. As we talked and laughed, I felt the baby kick and grabbed Chance's hand and held it to my round tummy. We sat for a moment and Chance's eyes went wide when he felt for the first time our little baby kick.

"Oh my god, does it hurt?" He asked in amazement.

"No, it feels weird but it doesn't hurt at all my Alpha." I replied.

He sat still and basked in the joy of feeling our little one, while I closed my eyes and just enjoyed his amazement. After an hour we were starting to get up. Chance held out his hand and lifted my struggling pregnant self-up off the ground with ease. Then we heard it and it made us both jump. BAM, thunder echoed through the silent mountainside as we felt our very insides jump at the deafening sound. Chance looked at me and I met his gaze as our minds thought back to Olma's cryptic warning. We began to head back to the house as fast as I could move. I did pretty well cause before long we made it inside when the clouds darkened the skies and rain began to fall hard against the roof.

Jonah looked at me and said "Do you think this is it, I mean you heard the thunder. Is that how it begins I wonder?" He asked in concern.

I don't know Chance but, this is an oddly intense storm for this time of year." I replied with the same concern he felt.

"Stay inside and lock the door behind me, my Omega. I love you babe, no matter what happens always know that." Then he ran out the door as I yelled his name in protest but, he disappeared into the shadows of the night. I held onto the fact he was so strong he could face down anything but my faith wavered when I thought of the figure of death. I shivered as I started the gas fireplace and sat in front of it fearfully awaiting his return. An hour passed then two as my frazzled nerves gave way to tears of fear.

Suddenly a banging came from the door and my body jerked in response to the unexpected sound. I ran to the door praying it was Chance but to my shock and disappointment it was Jase. My body tensed and my heart skipped a beat as my mind went wild, fearing he came to tell me my Alpha was dead.

"My Omega, I came to let you know Chance is fine, he is helping the boys secure the perimeter and he'll be gone half the night." Jase hollered through the loud roar of the storm.

"Thanks Jase, I was freaking the fuck out thinking the worst but, you've help me more than you know." I replied graciously.

"I am glad I could put your mind at ease my Omega." He stated as he backed away and disappeared in the darkness of the storm.

I laid on the soft couch and hours must have passed before I slowly drifted off into the comfort t of my dreams.

I awoke suddenly at the clap of the front door latching. It was Chance, joy filled my soul and I lumped to my feet and ran to him wrapping my arms around him as tears of relief wet my face.

"I was so afraid I would never see you again my Alpha!" I softly whispered into his ear.

"I'm fine baby, calm down, I will never leave you, not even if death itself came to claim me. I love you." He said, soothing my frayed nerves.

9. Chance

I cooked my Omega's breakfast as I felt a sense of anger and frustration fill my gut. Part of me wanted this vision of the future to be over and done. I knew now though, that it was still coming and I felt helpless to stop it. How was I going to protect my Omega if I didn't even know what was coming to kill us all?

I had just finished cooking his omelet when he emerged from the bedroom with a yawn and a smile. That beautiful smile was just what I needed to tear me away from my dark thoughts. I set the plate on the table in front of him and kissed his gorgeous face as I sat down beside him.

"What, you're not eating babe?" He asked me.

"No baby I have too much on my mind right now. I'll be sure to eat lunch though babe." I said in a comforting tone.

Ok, I'll be sure you do baby." He said with a mischievous smile.

I got up and went for my morning run hoping that it would help to ease my mind. However, when I returned home, I was still on edge and my Omega could sense it. He cautiously approached me and looked up into my haunted eyes and said, "Baby whatever is bothering you, you know you can tell me and I might be able to help."

I sighed conceding to the fact I needed someone to talk to. "I am just so worried that whatever this darkness is that's coming for us all will take you and our child from me."

He looked me deep in the eyes and flashed that beautiful smile again and said," My sweet Alpha, Nothing and no one will ever come between us again, not even death can separate us. I refuse to leave this world unless we are together."

Strangely that eased my frantic mind. I pulled him to me and held him tight in my arms breathing in his scent. Then I knelt down and kissed his round tummy.

"In about a month and a half we'll have a little one to care for baby." Anton said, then he asked," I hate to bother you with this but I need to go to town and get my prescriptions I'm almost out again but, this time the doctor called in a three-month supply so we won't have to worry about it again."

I smiled at him and said, "Of course baby, we can go as soon as you're ready."

Anton went into the bedroom and changed his clothes. We climbed into the truck and hit the road. Anton got lost in the beauty of the forest and lovely scenery of the early fall weather. It was a beautiful day. It seemed like they arrived in town, in no time at all, Anton thought. He had been so distracted. They pulled into the parking lot and came to a stop just outside the pharmacy. I said, "I'll be right back." Anton yanked his seatbelt off saying, "There is no way in hell I'm sitting in this truck waiting to be snatched by some fucking backwoods hillbillies again. I'm coming with you."

"Great, I'd like that." I said with a smile.

A short while later we came out saying, "Fucking roadside robbery, prescriptions should not be that expensive."

I saw the men's clothing store and said, "Babe, let's get you something to wear, you can't fit any of your clothes anymore."

He looked at me with excitement and said, "Ok, that sounds like a great plan." Then smiled at me as I held the door open for him.

He immediately went for the men's maternity section, obviously exclusively for Omegas so, I kept watch on everyone and let him go nuts. I really didn't like the idea of him being off of pack territory in his condition because it made him a target for hunters.

Knowing hunters scoped out places like this, I kept a close eye on everyone trying to see faces. This way I could recognize anyone who snuck up on us.

After about an hour he had several items chosen after trying them on so, I walked him to the checkout and payed. His eyes were wild with excitement and that made it all worth it.

We made it home around dusk and I didn't think we were followed, but if we were my wolves would catch them way before they got near my Omega.

He ran into the bedroom and told me to wait on the couch so he could show me everything. He proudly came out in some pretty nice fitting jeans they looked amazing on his hard ass. And a diesel shirt that really hid his waist you couldn't even see he was pregnant. After showing me everything he bought he came out in some sweats that had a very elastic waist band and a string to make them fit event the biggest tummy. I knew Anton wasn't there yet he had plenty of growing to do. I was just soaking in everyday I could, watching his tummy grow with the new life we had made together. I was the most incredible feeling, then suddenly the howls of alarm echoed in my ears and Anton stiffened. Anton looked at me and said, "Don't you dare." But I had to go and see who had crossed into pack territory.

"Baby I'll be back as soon as I find out who it is on pack land. I promise I won't be long." I said with a grimace.

Anton just shook his head and I knew I was in for it later but, I had to check and make sure they weren't hunters.

I transformed and made it to the northwest border in a minute or less and when I stepped close enough, I noticed the boys had someone tied up on the ground.

"Who are you and what are you doing on my packs territory." I growled angrily.

"The young man no older than nineteen looked up at me and his eyes caught my attention. I shook it off, I could smell the wolf but something was different and it reminded me of my Omega. Then he replied, "Forgive me Alpha, I meant no disrespect but, my brother, I heard he was here now and I have to see him. Please Alpha."

Brother huh? I thought to myself. Maybe that's why his eyes looked so familiar. I thought for a moment and said, "Jase, make sure this young pup is tied up properly, there's no way he's approaching my

Omega otherwise." Then I lead us down the hillside and along the trail to the large meeting ground in front of our home. I howled for Anton and he came out slowly. I yanked the pup out from the back and held his face tightly in my hand and asked, "If you do not know this pup then he is a dead little wolf." I growled even deeper now. I could feel the little man tremble.

Anton took one look and yelled Jason? Oh my god Jason, what are you doing here? How did you get free? He asked and then he ran to the little wolf and I backed away. Then Anton reached for the ropes and I jumped in saying, Whoa, whoa, babe what's happening? Is this really a brother of yours?"

My Omega replied, "Yes my only living relative, My little brother! Jase untie him please now!" He barked.

Jase started to glance at me but Anton reasserted, "Now Jase!"

"Yes, my Omega." Jase replied and he untied the boy and gave me a questioning look. I just shrugged and Followed Anton and the boy into the house.

I grabbed the whiskey bottle and leaned against the arm of the recliner while Anton questioned the kid. "So, how did you get away from your owners?"

"They weren't smart big brother!" he said laughing, then a sad look overtook him, the same look Anton had when we first met. "They, w-well they forced themselves on me, hoping that by doing that it would speed my cycle like it is said to do with some of our kind. But it didn't work so they just left me caged in the garage and threw scraps at me. They hosed me down with ice cold water every few days. I had to live in my own filth Anton." Cried the boy. I saw the heartbreak in my Omega's eye's again as he held his little brother and they cried together. I suddenly felt ashamed for my rough handling of the young man and got up to make them dinner.

I made sure it was a big meal because not only did I have Anton to care for but his little brother also. It broke my heart the more I noticed how malnourished the young Omega was. Even worse than my Omega when I first saw him.

I called to them, letting them know dinner was ready. The young man was fast I'll give him that. "So, Jason, right? I asked in a gentle tone.

Y-Yes Alpha." He replied fearfully.

"Jason you're my little brother now and I see it as my responsibility to care for you and protect you as part of my pack and my family. Please don't be afraid of me. I would never hurt you man" I said with a wide smile and a playful tap on his shoulder. He seemed to relax a little and I went into the kitchen to grab their plates. "Well, we have ribeye steak, mashed potatoes with gravy, steamed broccoli and side salads. Then we're having chocolate cake with cream cheese frosting."

Jason's eyes got wide and his mouth hung half open as I put the plate in front of him and sat to eat. He looked at the food, then at me. I said, "Dig in Jason buddy, we have to fatten you up a little." And smiled at him.

He tore into it with a grin and fevered look in his eyes. He gobbled up the massive plate of food and patiently waited on desert. I got up when my Omega said he was full and went to cut the cake. I came back with a large slice for Jason and he gobbled that down while I made up the spare bedroom with fresh linens and a duvet.

I dug through a box of clothes my cousin had left behind and found some clothes I thought would fit him. He looked shocked when I gave them to him. I showed him to the second bathroom and he showered then, I showed him the large room and bed making sure he understood it was all his and he began to cry. Then he turned those emerald eyes on me and wrapped his scrawny arms around me and said, "Thank you, Alpha." I gently hugged him patting his boney back and said, "It's all yours as long as you want it Jason. It's your home too now."

He turned his head embarrassed to cry in front of his new Alpha and said "Thank you Alpha, I've never had a bed of my own before." Then he smiled up at me. Even though it broke my heart I smiled back and said goodnight.

10. Anton

It had been a week and Jason seemed to be getting better. Chance had him eating three meals and several snacks every day to build up his strength and put some weight on him.

It was nice to see Jason taking after Chance in so many ways. He seemed to be gleaning all of Chance's finest qualities. That, somehow made me feel much more confident he could get past the scars of the past. Chance has been my beacon in the dark night and he is for Jason now, as well. It made me love my Alpha all the more.

I've never met a man like Chance before. He's so very kind and loving but also fierce when it came to his family and his pack. I had every confidence he would be a wonderful father to our baby.

I also knew Chance was struggling with elder Olma's vision and trying his hardest to hide it. It seems I have a mate who fears the future and a little brother who fears his past. I had no idea how to help either one of them but I was determined to try.

Jason being nineteen and about to turn twenty couldn't help but be curious about what to expect when his body was ready to father a child. I tried my very best to explain, his cycle could start during his twenties but most likely around twenty-one. I explained the symptoms of being in the midst of a cycle and how miserable it can make your body feel, how sexually aroused it can make you around males, especially Alpha's.

Chance and I had talked earlier about getting Jason some new clothes that actually fit him. So, when Chance walked in the door he Called for Jason and then told him he was going to take him shopping. I let them know I was tired (being just over four months into my six-month pregnancy) and would be staying home to rest. It was so endearing the way Jason looked up to Chance and even tried to mimic his behavior in several ways. Jason and I never really knew our father very well except the he was cruel and he was a shitty person so he was a bad influence.

The day my father sold me, my mother killed herself and Jason was the one who found her hanging from a beam in the garage. That day was the last day I saw either one of the only two people I loved in the world at the time. Jason was just sixteen when my father sold me and I know at that young age, seeing our mother like that must have horrified him. I had asked him about that day two days ago and he just said "Please Anton, I can't." And I didn't press the question, I knew he'd open up when he was ready.

After Chance and Jason left to go shopping, I went and laid down in our bed. I must have fallen asleep very quickly. I began to dream It was a beautiful fall night and the full moon shown bright and brilliant in the night sky. The pack was gathered at the meeting grounds outside the house and one by one they began to shift into werewolf form. Then fire emerged like a living being from the trees and started to walk towards the center of the meeting grounds burning to a crisp anyone who stood in its path. I heard sounds of thunder all around me and I could see bodies everywhere. Then suddenly, Chance is holding me telling, "It's all right babe. Just relax. I've got you."

My eyes opened wide and I felt strange. It was all so very real, like I was there. "I need to talk to Olma." I stated.

Chance replied, "Ok, babe anything, just relax."

They headed to Olma's house and like usual the door opened and Olma greeted us at the door.

"Come in, I was expecting to hear from you." Olma said with a smile.

 "I need to tell you something and I want you to tell me what it means." I said.

I rattled off all that had come to me in my dream and how it felt. That it felt so real. She leaned in and sniffed my shoulder and then touched my tummy and leaned back with a smile.

"Ahhh, this vision did not come from you, you do not have the sight. It came from the pup growing within you. This child will be blessed with many gifts." Olma said with a nod.

"What does that mean, elder Olma?" I asked but she just replied with," Everything will reveal itself in due time young one."

On the drive back to our house I was obviously distracted and Chance could tell. He put his hand on my leg and said in a gentle tone, "It's going to be fine babe, I promise, just relax a bit ok. All this worrying can't be good for the baby."

"I know, I'm sorry it's just all so strange. I can't make heads or tails out of it." I replied but decided I needed to change my focus or I would just dwell on it.

We arrived home and Went into the house and saw Jason playing a video game on the TV. I smiled as Chance went to join him, they laughed and just had a great time. While they were playing, I looked at how he treated Jason and a feeling of peace swept over me. This big strong man, My Alpha loved us and was provided for us. He truly was our rock and protector.

I could barely defend myself being pregnant, it stops your ability to shift so, I was stuck in human form for the entirety of my pregnancy.

Jason deserved happiness growing up he was so gentle and sweet it broke his little heart every time our father would slap us or hurt mother. Our father was a horrible, hate filled person but Chance, He would be a wonderful father. Jason was continuing to gain weight and his muscle was returning, becoming more defined. He really was getting stronger, probably healthier than he's ever been.

I made my way to the couch and Chance lost a life on the video game helping me sit without flopping, my tummy was getting so big. My Alpha and my brother getting along so well, made my heart swell.

It gave me some comfort knowing that if something happened to me, they would have each other to turn to. This pregnancy was high risk after all. I had no idea what I was doing in this situation but, I had to believe it was the right thing to do.

11. Jason

I couldn't help but space out once in a while and think about the situation I had escaped from. There was only one person in that bunch that worried me. Leathan, he was the one man in that group that really scared me. Could my new Alpha protect me from such a powerful warlock?

When my Alpha and I returned from our morning run, we ran into Jase.

Jase nodded at his Alpha, "Chance," Then Jase glanced at me and cleared his throat, "My Alpha, I have a lead on the family and Ryan thinks they'll make a move soon." My Alpha nodded and went into the house.

I couldn't help but notice Jase. He smiled at me and winked when he passed by me. Oh, I could just picture that one with nothing but his underwear on. He was older but, still close to my age and he was into me. I could tell. He had beep blue sapphire eyes and nicely cut blonde hair. His muscles rippled under everything he wore. Oh god, he was at least six feet tall, built and gorgeous.

I had to shake those thoughts away If I was ever going to find a way to tell my Alpha who I escaped from. I can never seem to find the right moment and every time I think it's a good time something comes and makes it a bad time.

But today, looked like a good day to spill, nothing was going on and I was feeling pretty nervous. After we finished lunch, I looked at my Alpha and lowered my head I tried my hardest to sound normal.

"My Alpha?" I managed.

"Yeah Jason, what's up buddy?" He replied.

I struggled for a moment then I said," I have to tell you something about the people I ran from."

"I know about them Jason and that they have a pack sorcerer." My Alpha said just as calm and cool as could be.

"My Alpha. He's very powerful, no matter what, don't underestimate him and what he's capable of." I stated as fast as possible.

"Thanks Jason but when I end up facing him and I know I will, I will destroy him. Now stop letting this trouble you buddy." Said my Alpha calmly with a touch of arrogance. That's what scared me, that my Alpha would be caught unawares by this warlock because of overconfidence.

Around dinner time I was standing out on the back patio taking in the view when howls came from the hillside. I couldn't understand the howls, it was code or something. My Alpha came bursting out the back door and answered in another coded howl. One more howl and he stood tall at the base of the back patio just waiting. Then they came out of the trees one of the guard patrols and they had someone in tow.

"Alpha." the men said. Then Jase came to the front and handed my Alpha a camera, with a major lens on it. When my Alpha looked at the pictures, he started to growl low as thunder and I stepped back. His claws and canines extended and he pulled the man to his feet then up close to his face.

"Do you desire a slow death or a quick one." He asked the man.

"I-I- W- would like to not die. If at all possible." The man cried.

"Then explain what my family is doing in these pictures?" He asked with a snarl.

"I was told to get pictures of the people close to you that's it, I swear!" The man bellowed.

"By whom?" Who asked you to spy for them?" He asked the man angrily.

"Leathan! His name's Leathan, he's the Conner packs warlock. He'll kill me if he finds out I told you anything." Cried the man desperately.

"I know just what to do with this one." Said my Alpha as he hurried off with the guards.

I went inside and saw Anton just inside the doorway. He turned to me and asked.

"What about this Warlock is so frightening? Do you really believe he can kill Chance?"

"I pray not, but, he's more powerful than anyone I've ever met and he's sick, he's insanely cruel." I answered fearfully.

"Why does he frighten you so badly? What are you not saying Jason?" Anton said intensely.

"He was the one who tried to get me to conceive, he forced himself on me more than once." I said it all before the tears could come, but they did come.

Anton held me as I cried and told me how much he loved me. How he wished it could have been different for me. I forced myself to calm down and decided to go lie down. I was tired from all the stress over telling my Alpha but, also from stress knowing they have figured out where I am. I know for a fact also; he's definitely going to want my pregnant brother.

12. Chance

I held Anton close to me and he shifted a little and rubbed his ass against my package. Oh man, the head of my hardening flesh twitched at the sensation of him and he felt it, turned over and smiled at me then he leaned in and kissed me deep and overpoweringly. I could smell the aroma of arousal he put off and it made me yearn for him. I stopped and asked, "What about the baby?"

"The doctor said, sex was actually good for my body and my hormones." He replied with a playful grin.

I just beamed wide and got up and shut the door to our bedroom. As I slowly made my way to the bed, I did a slow strip tease for him. Taking off one piece of clothing at a time until the air was dense with our awakening craving. I moved up the bed and dragged his underwear off and smelled them as I tossed them over my shoulder. I moved up his inner thigh and felt his erection convulse as my hot breath passed over it. I couldn't hold back I immersed his hard erection my longing mouth and he moaned in delight. I swirled my tongue around its head and then licked my way down his shaft, over his balls, to his tight portal, now wet with yearning. I licked at it and the taste of his moisture made a low sensual rumble slowly arise from my chest.

I spread his legs and fully occupied his tight rosette with my mouth working it and penetrating it with my tongue. He moaned, having been worked into a frenzy.

I ran my tongue up his tummy and stopped to kiss it then up his neck to his ravenous mouth. My tongue entangled his in a feverish kiss. I gently worked him onto his side and slowly pressed my engorged cock against his dilating rosette from behind. He growled a hungry growl and I pressed inside as he arched in pleasure. I was mad with longing; we hadn't enjoyed each other like this since Jason arrived and I was aching for the intimacy of my lover.

I rhythmically penetrated deep in and then out in slow waves of ever-increasing frenzied thrusts. I needed him, I loved him and he was my everything. I slowly kissed at his back as I pleasured his tight portal. He began to rub his own hard member so, I moved tight against him and reached around to pleasure his manhood as my own peak of ecstasy rose to the surface. My knot started to form. I struggled to keep going until I felt his cock spasm as he reached back and grabbed my ass. Arching his back, he began to squirt torrents of his hot white essence and I Groaned deeply as I spilled inside.

We laid there and I embraced my Omega as I kissed the back of his neck. I laid my hand on his tummy and felt the baby kick. I was in heaven. "I love you my sweet Omega, nothing and no one will separate the four of us babe I swear to you. You, the baby and Jason are my dear family and I will protect you all with my life."

The next morning Jase knocked then popped his head in and said, "Hey sorry My Omega but I need Chance, is he available it's really important."

Anton replied, "Sure, give me a sec."

When I got to the door and Jase gave me that hurry up look so, I jogged to the door and Jase pulled me outside.

"Shit Chance this is bad man, look." Jase said. As he told me These pictures have been uploaded to a secure server. We don't know exactly where but its local." Jase said worry in his voice.

As I looked through the pictures, I saw he had several of Anton my mate and his pregnant tummy. My mind began to swim. If he was trying to get Jason pregnant, what will he do now that he knows an Omega is already expecting right here.

"Double the boundary patrols and make sure nobody gets near Jason or my mate! This warlock is coming and we need to be ready." I said in a very stern voice.

"Yes, my Alpha, we'll be ready, nobody is getting past us!" Jase said confidently.

The afternoon gave way to dusk and then the unforgiving black of night. We all sat around unable to sleep and Anton had gone to the bedroom for a while then came back and said,

" If you need to be out there Chance, go. We'll be fine baby." Anton said.

I walked up to my handsome Omega and kissed his cheek saying," Ok baby, I'll howl if anything goes wrong."

Anton smiled and I secured the door behind me. I made it to the boundary patrols and talked with Jase he said scouts have seen nothing and all is quiet. Something though, it just didn't sit right with me. So, I made my way back down the hill to the center of the gathering area. I sensed an unfamiliar odor like ozone and sulfur. I tuned and my chest felt like I had been hit with a hammer and I flew a few feet landing on my feet sliding backwards with a growl. I lifted my head and howled to the others.

"So, you think you can take my family away do you? I'll eat your throat out first mage!" I screamed in disgust.

"Oh, do stop barking, you're quite the exhausting one aren't you? From this angle however, you're of no consequence." Said Leathan and with a wave of his hand I was frozen. The others though burst through the trees and surrounded him. He laughed and vanished. Reappearing behind me and pulling an athame out and holding it against my exposed throat.

Then suddenly a flash of light blinding and white cracked through the night and Leathan winced, "You should leave creature before I grow tired of your ranting." Leathan dropped the blade and turned shakily to the voice of our pack elder Olma.

"You can't be hear, how? No matter, I will be back and I will have what's mine!" Leathan screamed and vanished into thin air.

Olma smiled as she approached me. "Young Alpha, I will be ready for Leathan when he returns but I fear he will not return alone. He will bring his minions his wolf pack with him and I'm certain, some additional abominations I will, no doubt, have to dispatch." Then she patted my shoulder and walked into the night towards her home.

My fettered nerves couldn't take anymore damned surprises. I made my way up the steps and as I walked in my family all ran to me. Anton and Jason wrapped their arms around me. This, right here, was what I was fighting to keep and what I was so afraid to lose.

The next morning, I ran the perimeter with Jase. We stopped about twenty miles into the run to catch our breath. Jase asked me when the last time was Anton and I had a romantic evening just the two of us.

The fact I was thinking about it was clear indication it had been too long. I had an idea a three-day trip at one of the fanciest resorts around. So, for the next three quarters of the run my mind raced as I mulled over all the potential romantic hot spots. I couldn't make up my mind, until it occurred to me that rustic, he had in his home, so go upscale. After I got home from my run, I made a few calls and I had just the place lined up. It was only forty-five minutes away and incredible.

13. Anton

Chance had told me to get out my fancy clothes and I thought something was up but I played dumb. I just knew he had a plan to go somewhere fun.

About two hours later I finally had my shower, dressed and had my stuff picked out. At last I was ready and waiting rather anxiously to go. Anxious I thought, he doesn't get anxious unless something nefarious was afoot. The scent of it didn't strike as being elusive. So, I just let it go and decided to just enjoy the ride where ever it takes me.

We drove about fifty minutes and the scenery was to die for the elegant seasonal change in the air. Yellows, oranges and reds with the occasional spot of brown it was brilliant, I could feel the colors they were so vibrant. We passed by the occasional field, filled with grazing deer of all ages. I only became aware after an occasional question from My love Chance or, the even less likely, sporadic pothole.

I was getting the idea we were there when he pulled off the highway onto what looked like a resort road "YES!" I knew he'd remembered." Were the words I found myself thinking when we pulled up to a huge resort. We arrived to the very busy front of the resort. I'd noticed the people were wearing Gucci, Couture and Armani and other names I couldn't pronounce, were the ones going in and out. Now I was the one with the elevated heart rate. The valet took his Keyes and the bellboy grabbed our luggage. Then the valet took the truck. As we walked in the fanciful gorgeousness took me by complete surprise. The chandelier was all glistening with lights dancing on the ceiling around it.

Borders around the ceiling were made of porcelain and white with gold plated designs twirling all about. We got up to the 98th floor and then the bell dinged again then stopped! The Penthouse! Yes! This gentleman of mine is actually completely perfect. He carried out the luggage and made his way to the front door and the host with the room key handed Chance the key and received a very generous tip. I walked up to him and he held me in front of the glass wall overlooking an enormous river and the forested hills so perfectly with the crescent moon partially obscured by the tree tops.

He looked deep into my eyes and said" I love you Anton my Omega with every fiber of my being, I love you. Happy six-month anniversary my love."

Oh my god He's scoring so high in the romantic chart tonight. The attendant bowed slightly at the front door. It made me realize so, I ran up to him and gave him a nice tip. Then he and handed Chance the dinner reservations, graciously accepted the tip and backed out.

I was overtaken by the exquisiteness of my surroundings. The chandelier and the white carpet that shimmered every color of the rainbow. The crimson couch had the most wonderful material. There was a bar filled with exotic liquors. The kitchen floors were custom ceramic tiles and marble countertops that glowed in the dark.

The master sweet had a huge canopy bed and antique desk (if there's one thing I'm good at its spotting an antique) made of maple. It had a twelve by twelve walk in closet that had a safe with biometric scanner. The bathroom suite off the master bedroom was unbelievable. A two person walk in shower and a jacuzzi. Out on the patio it had a pool and a hot tub. With a climate-controlled solarium with every stunning exotic plant you could ever envision sprites and lights danced all around as if excited to see me.

I looked at him and said, "I have nothing to wear in a place like this!"

Chance replied, "I thought you might say that so I scheduled you with two hours at the men's clothing on the third floor." I was so excited I couldn't wait to put on some of the clothes at this place. We arrived at the store and the employees immediately walked up and said, "Is this the famous Anton?"

I smiled and said "yes."

They came out like a whirlwind and started showing me what shirt to go with what pants and what shoes go with what pants. I was so overjoyed by the pampering being almost five months pregnant and due in a month to six weeks this was heaven not having to struggle through decisions. They would gladly throw in opinions and it would be a perfect outfit every time.

After I had about six new outfits that would be altered after the baby comes, trust me.

 Chance held out his arm and led me to an amazing dining room. Each table had flowers, bioluminescent flowers. A ceiling that looked like the nights sky. I was in amazement. Chance took my hand and led me to our table and the server announced the specials, then backed away.

"I can't believe this baby, It's all so amazing. I've never been anywhere like this." I said ardently.

The server returns with their assorted world cheeses and wine whit a bottle (nonalcoholic) grape champagne. Then he took their orders and swiftly brought their drinks. Finally, alone. He gazed into me and I began to blush. I smiled and said," What?"

He just replied, "I love you so much baby happy six-month anniversary my Omega." As he leaned in to kiss him those two seconds lasted and eternity, because I had to fucking pee bad and now!

I jumped up and said, "bathroom be right back."

When I got back, I was actually calm and having a great time. I couldn't believe what this must have cost last minute for three days? Wow he does love me. Dinner took two and a half hours and even though the portions are small they add up to a lot. I loved every course though, wow.

We made it to the suite and into the jacuzzi long day driving excitement and now this. The relaxing bubbles tickled and made beautiful magical colors because the bath bubbles were magical bubble bath soap.

The next day they went on a helicopter ride and went to get lunch at some fancy middle eastern deli, which was delicious. Then we hit the shops downtown and passed by several day walking vampires. That was strange because the amulet or charm that is spelled to protect them from the sun are always very rare and expensive and they run out of juice the more you use it.

Our third day was relaxation day so, we went down for a massage. I was incredible and I asked the attendant if they had a chiropractor on the resort too. laughing. She looked and said yes. I just said, "Thank you." and we walked away laughing.

14. The beginning of the end

Chance askes, "Jase, how's Jason doing man?"

"He seems alright but then he has terrible nightmares." Jase answers.

"Yeah, he's gonna have a tough time with this but, he's fierce inside his wolf is powerful, he'll bounce back man, I just see him coming more and more alive every day. "Chance states.

"What was that Jase?" Chance looks at Jase with suspicion. You're nervous Jase." Why?"

"B-Because I asked him on a date ok. C'mon Chance I'm a gentleman you know that and we're only four years apart? Plus, he's so handsome." Jase asked with conviction.

"Fine, but, Mind yourself." Chance warned.

Jase did a skip and a jump and hurried down the patio steps. Jason following close behind from around back.

"See ya Jase." Chance looks at him and turns with a smile.

I walked up behind my mate and grabbed him by his waist placing each hand on the sides of his tummy feeling our little angel move and kick. "What's it feel like?" Chance asked.

"Well it feels like your tummy flutters and that's it really, I mean sometimes he can kick a sensitive spot and it hurts a tiny bit but, otherwise It feels amazing! We're close to the due date baby, a month to go." Anton said smiling wide. Chance's smile just got even brighter.

They started a bath and Chance and Anton got in together. They just figured they'd give Jason and Jase more time to smooch on each other. Which they certainly took advantage of,

" Oh god Jase you're so amazing, I just love kissing you." Murmured Jason.

I love your body and your gorgeous face and just you." Jase smiles and then the idea of what he just said came raining down on him.

But before he could get a word out Jason interrupts saying, "Nobody has ever loved me, do you mean it Jase?"

"Of course, I do, I want you to be mine, and if you change your mind later, you will still be free to mate with someone else. You just have to remember that a werewolf life mates once and then is single forever, ok?" Jase said.

"Um hello Jase, I'm a werewolf too man and I'm getting strong see? and he flashed his very well-defined arms and abs.

Jase replied, "I-I-uh-um-see man, god you're so hot." And back to kissing they went.

The moment became a little too much when Jase held Jason against the wall and started to go down on him, "Wo, wo, I need time. I can't I'm sorry." Jason said sincerely.

No, I'm sorry I always push too fast, how about I see you tomorrow?" Jase asked.

"Great Jase, I'll keep my books open." They both chuckle and Jase hops in his truck and heads home.

Looks like Jase finally gave up and went home." Chance said smiling wide.

"Yeah, I just hope that Jase can respect what Jason has been through and waits before coming on too strong." Anton says in concern. "Plus, I don't need one of your Betas corrupting my little brother." Anton says playfully.

"I don't think I ever told you but, Jase comes from Alpha blood.

I didn't want you to know so you wouldn't leave me for another Alpha." Chance says as they both laugh and tickle at one another.

"His family stepped aside generations ago because my family's alpha lineage was stronger and better fit to lead." Chance stated.

Out of nowhere they hear the patrols howling in the distance and Chance leaps to his feet. "The perimeter has been breached and there's a panic something they are afraid of." Chance says startled.

Chance help Anton get out of the tub and rushes to get dressed." Lock the door behind me baby. I'll send men to keep you and Jason safe!" Chance said as he frantically struggled to dress while wet.

15. Endgame

Chance gets outside and see's Jase they meet up and shift to werewolf form with long clawed arms and legs pointed ears and covered in thick fur. Chance said let's check this out. They leap through the trees and forest like monkeys and make it to an opening to the sight of fire. Relentlessly walking and they seemed to be wielding flaming swords?

"Are you seeing this Jase?" Chance asked in confusion.

"We need to get Olma NOW!" Jase said "This is magic!"

They went to get Elder Olma and Find another beast made of fire approaching the pack meeting grounds. The pack was assembling and shifting to werewolf form. They were running to get rocks and fallen trees to hurl at the mysterious creatures made of fire and black glass. Each arial assault was trumped by the swing of the flaming swords, they seemed to cut through even solid stone. They hacked at the trees until they came to the clearing

Leathan appears out of nowhere hovering in the air and laughing. "You see Alpha? I will have my omega's, both of them and the child is mine so give up now and I'll spare some of your people." Leathan states maniacally.

"NEVER! You will not touch my family, dark sorcerer!" Chance screams.

"Oh, and who will stop me? You little Alpha?" Leathan says.

"No Leathan, it will be me." Olma states calmly.

Chance doesn't know the extent of Olma's power but surely a priestess can't be a match for a warlock! He thought to himself.

"The Fire elementals will die first. Then you, Leathan. I warned you to never harm my protected and you have chosen to ignore my gracious warning." Olma says with a hint of anger. "Now is the time for your judgment."

The second fire elemental emerges from the burning trees and Olma Points to them both and screams a magic word. Blue silvery beams shoot from her hands drizzling snowflakes as they collide with the fire elementals. In a massive explosion of steam and the deafening sounds of snapping and cracking the elementals both begin to freeze into ice and crumble.

Then the sounds of thunder clapping begin to echo through the forest as shooters in the trees (who used the elementals as a distraction) begin to fire upon the unsuspecting werewolves. Chance howls for them to take out the shooters as wolf after wolf falls dead from the lethal snipers.

"The snipers are from the pack members looking for Jason and Anton!" Jase yelled.

"Ok, let's focus on the shooters, Olma's got this warlock."

Olma's visage melts away to reveal a beautiful elven mage glowing with power and clad in blue silk draping from her now floating form.

"You cannot best me mortal, I beseech you to stop all this at once and let peace be the victor." Olma states wistfully.

"I will best you woman and kill every last one of your pets too!" Leathan laughs wickedly.

He speaks ancient words and lightning shoots at Olma but with a wink of her eye a shield dissipates the blast. Then suddenly she sees it the specter of death from her vision, Dark and foreboding. Weaving through the crowd dropping death on whoever it touches.

"You fool Leathan! You have bound an angel of death to you to use as your puppet!" Olma exclaims in shock. She can see the magical tether holding the being enslaved. Olma protects some of the pack's women and children from one of Leathan's fiery blasts. Then she pulls at nature, pooling her own power into a ball of white magic and hurls it at Leathan, sending him spiraling into a large tree and landing to the ground with a huff. He leans up and inhales a gasp after having the wind knocked out of him.

Chance and Jase make their way up the trees one after the other ripping and slicing snipers one after the other until the last is dead. Then from high up in the tree Chance can see the back windows of their home had been broken out. He screams at Jase, "Jase the house, Anton and Jason need us NOW!"

They both bolt down the trail of massive trees and pounce onto the back patio. They carefully climb through the broken-out windows. They can hear yelling. Jase peeks around a corner as someone yells, "You god damned dog!" Then the man punches Anton in the face sending him to the ground. Jase instantly leaps into the living room as the man pulls a machete and goes on the defensive.

"How dare you even touch my Omega, pig!" Jase growls as Chance comes up to Anton to check on him.

Jase is standing off with the human hunter. In a whirl of blade and claws the men go round and round until the man catches Jase's side with the blade cutting deep, but Jase stands strong.

The man catches Jase's shoulder and laughs then his grin fades as his head falls to the ground. Chance squares off with the other one and the man swings the blade catching Chances arm but, Chance take the opportunity to strike and strike he did. His claws and hand sink deep into the man's stomach dragging out intestines with his now closed fist.

Olma deflects glittering magical strikes and propels her own version of magic as vines creep from the ground and catch the warlock around the ankles, then his hands and finally he is bound in such a way he cannot cast spells.

Chance and Anton along with Jason and Jase make it outside to escape the now burning house. The warlock Leathan still has the angel of death and all he needs is to think his commands. Then death turns its attention on the four of them and slowly makes his way over to them. Olma looks at the warlock and cries, "Leathan stop, please you cannot!"

Leathan winks one eye and the shadowy angel vanishes and appears behind them touching Anton's shoulder and Chance looks at Anton lifeless eyes as his body grows limp and falls dead to the ground.

Chance howls in pain and scoops him up onto his lap on the ground and sobs.

"Oh, god no! No baby you can't leave me! I need you more than anything, my reason for breathing, you're the reason for everything I live for!" Chance cried.

Olma looks at Leathan and says I'm sorry old warlock but a life for a life, we need to keep the balance. She points to the angel of death and recites an ancient spell the tether between the spirit and Leathan lights up a bright red and Olma concentrates harder pulling on the magical tether with all the strength she can gather. The tether begins to glow white hot and with a blinding flash it explodes into a shower of sparks.

Before the angel can leave Olma says, "WAIT spirit!" In a commanding voice, "You have committed a great evil and though it is not of your doing, it is up to you to make it right, you will restore the balance by putting life back into those that you have stolen it from."

The now white form bows and with a wave of his hand all the fallen wolfs that were taken by death begin to wake up. Except for Anton.

"What is this? What's happening here why isn't he waking up. The angel solidifies and raises his face to meet their gaze, "He is walking the spirit realm. I cannot bring him back if he will not return."

"How can I talk to him?" Chance pleads.

"You need only speak and he will perceive your words child." The angel replies.

"Anton, baby please if you can hear me, I love you so much, I need you so much baby. Your brother Jason needs you and you have our baby inside you my Omega. None of us are a family without you baby, you're the glue that keeps us all together. I love you. Please babe!" Chance whispered in desperation.

Then Anton's finger twitches and he says in a weak voice, "This is where I get CPR." And everyone bursts out in much needed laughter.

Olma breaks in with" And your captor angel, what of him?"

"I will care for this being myself." And snaps his fingers as the warlock screams and vanishes into a puff of white smoke.

16 Picking up the pieces

Olma having shed her disguise told us about a pact she had made with the pack's ancestors a thousand years ago to forever watch over and protect them.

Jason had suffered little injury and my Omega healed very fast from his beating. The baby was fine and due any day now. Jase and Jason have been seeing each other every night for a while now and I think they really complement each other. We had the forest sprites heal all the burnt trees that made it through the fire and the forest floor as well. Things were not only getting back to normal but Anton and Jason no longer had to fear their past captors aver again. The relief was so apparent on them they were both happier and freer than I've ever seen them.

Anton picked a box up off the couch and stopped. Our werewolf bond was getting stronger and I felt his pain and ran to his side. "What is it babe, talk to me."

He just looked me in the eye's and said, "This is it."

What's it?" I asked totally clueless.

"This is it, baby." He said

I looked at him confused and he glanced at his big tummy and back at me and I stared blankly like a deer in the headlights then ---CLICK! My brain kicked in, "OH my god baby! Hey guys let's go its baby time!

Jason says, "I'll get the bag and Jase get the truck."

As the truck pulled up to the front door, we all piled in and Olma gave us a wave and a nod. We arrived at the hospital about twenty minutes later and We walked in, I was doting all over my Omega. He smiled at me and said, "baby, I'm fine, the baby's fine. Let's do this."

I followed into the hospital room and it was huge probably because my insurance was the best for my baby. The doctor came in and she said ok let's take a peek. Jason's was laying comfortably on his side and the doctor came in saying, "Ok on your back please Dad we need to check on the baby. She moved her hand down where I couldn't see then came back up saying, "Everything looks perfectly normal, the birth canal has opened completely and closed off everything else to make room for your little one. I give it two maybe three hours to go folks. Then she left and Anton just gazed into my eyes and said, "You're the love of my life and you saved me in every way possible, baby. You have forever changed me and taught me that love truly is a glorious gift." He said as I teared up. All I could manage was, "I love you too baby more than I can ever say." And we held each other then another contraction hit and I could feel him tense up. It slowly backed off and we had a moment of reprieve. Anton looked pale and I asked, "What is it baby? Are you ok?"

"Uh Chance my Alpha, you need to get the doctor this doesn't feel right!" Anton exclaimed.

I ran and got the nurse and she told the doctor. Within two minutes the doctor came in and said, Ok dad your blood pressure is dropping so we need you to really focus and stay awake, can you do that for me?" with a tight expression on her face. I mumbled the words I'm up, lets do this." With a smile.

She reached in between his legs and said, "Big push Anton you got this."

He pushed with all his might and then took a big breath. But the doctor said, "Ok Anton this baby needs to come now. The baby's oxygen is plummeting you need to push like you have nothing left in the world, but to push NOW!"

Anton bared down hard for what seemed like an entire minute

without a breath and then collapsed back as the sound of crying filled the tense air. "Chance Reynolds and Anton Winters, you, have a baby boy!"

We just smiled at one another. I held Anton as he held our little blue-eyed angel. The world was perfect in that moment and we would protect our baby from anyone and everything that might want to hurt him.

The alarms on the monitors started to sound and the doctors rushed in like a tornado and began shouting things I couldn't quite discern. Then they started to wheel Anton out and took him barreling down the hall to the operating room. I was panicked but, the nurse stayed behind to tell me he's hemorrhaging and they needed to stop the bleeding and give him blood. She asked if he had any family willing to donate. I said, "His brother."

"Perfect." she said, "He's an omega and his blood type is very rare we will need the brother, what's his name?" She asked calmly considering.

"Jason Winters. Is he going to be ok?" I pleaded.

"All I know is he's in the best hands right now and we have the best surgeons caring for him, So, just try and relax sir I know it's hard but it's all we can do." Sha stated calmly. It seemed to ease my nerves a tiny bit knowing he was in such good hands.

I held my baby until they had him cleaned up and wrapped him in a warm blanket. I took him out with me to meet Jase. As soon as I approached, he could smell my fear.

"What's wrong Chance why did they take Jason for blood?"

It's Anton. He's bleeding internally and they have to stop it and give him a transfusion. My god I don't know what I'll do without him." I stated, choking back my urge to cry.

"Anton's strong Chance and he's stubborn to boot so, he's got that on his side. He'll make it buddy." Jase reassured me as best he could, considering.

After about an hour the doctor came out and sighed," It looks like we were able to stop the bleeding just in time but he's anemic and weak. He's receiving the blood as fast as we can get it into him safely. He should be fine in a few days' sir, and congratulations.

I swear I almost burst into tears and probably would have but, Jase was there so I could never show weakness even to him.

A few days later we made it home and we put Little Brent Jase Winters Reynolds in his crib for the first time and he fell fast asleep. We all gathered in the living room as I made us martinis. After handing them out Chance toasted, "To Great family who are fierce and loving. Always there when you need someone. That are the best of friends and the most loving family, my most cherished individuals. Cheers."

We all held out our glasses and drank them down.

Later Jase came to me and asked if he had permission to see Jason on a more serious front than just the occasional date. I teased him saying, "You want him to go steady with you?" With a wicked grin on my face. Jase just laughed and said, "I'm serious Chance, I really am falling in love with him and want to pursue this. Will you give us your blessing as Alpha?"

"Of course, Jase, Anton and I both really trust you to be gentle with him and respect him. I know you will so, yes, my friend. "I said with a grin and a hug.

"Thanks Chance, I know it's hard for Anton to trust and tell him I really appreciate his faith in me." Jase told me with sincere gratitude.

We went back in to join the others and My Omega announced a group hug so we all stood in a circle. As we stood in a circle, we all put our arms around one another and held each other, breathing in the peace and happiness that was our family. We all knew that in this circle we would always find companionship, trust, strength and unwavering loyalty.

We were a family.

Epilogue

I can't believe Leathan is dead. He was one of the best of us. The mirror starts to flash up high in the right corner. It's the Union of assassins. The man in the suit waves his hand at the mirror and a lady on the other side of the mirror appears saying, "Come on stand up straight so I can see those eyes." The man corrects his posture and the mirror reflects only the man's eyes and then it returns to normal again.

"I am the agent transferring you to this contract 35 million $ for the complete destruction and deaths of Chance Reynolds, Anton Winters and child, Jason Winters and Jase Burrows. You have thirty days to complete this. If you fail you will be judged by the Union authority. Do you understand?" She states robotically.

"Yes Union, I understand." Leo replied.

"Good now place your hand on the mirror surface and complete the binding contract." The woman stated plainly.

When he placed his hand to the mirror it faded saying, "Thank you, sir, have a nice day."

Then the mirror returns to normal.

Well Looks like I had better get my traveling clothes on then shouldn't I. Then he smiles insidiously.

Acknowledgement

I have to acklowledge John my Editor and my mother for pushing me to work through the dissapointments (even though I wont let her red them) I love you both very much. Finally to Amazon for creating this inovative and easy to use system to puclish and be heard hats off to you amazon.

About The Author

Robert J. Morris

I am very new to all this and just decided one day to write my thoughts down. Then my partner said publish them on amazon so were we are. I would very much appreciate all my readers and other authers to read these works and help me with feedback please , much love.

Books In This Series

Werewolves of the West

This is a series that closely follow the lives of our heroes as their close knit family and friends grows through their adventures. They run into daik magicsand dangerous creatures not seen in centurys.Can they all survive until they can getto the bottom of these continuos assaults before falling prey to the attackers and their beasts?

Dicovering My Omega

Chance Reynolds is the wealthy 25 year old Alpha of a large pack in the Willamette National Forest. Anton Winters is a 25 year old lonely abused Omega who finds refuge in the arms of his new alpha. He also struggles to put the past behind him. Can they overcome the still haunting past that keeps coming to steal their happiness and love one another? Can they overcome and rise above the looming threats trying to steal their joy.

with his sexuality. Can he come to terms with it all and allow love in, or will he deny his new fate and his heart when all is said and done?

Infinit'y Embrace

It seems fate is not done with our three favorite couples Devon and Jonah--Ian and Denton—Rich and Mikael. As a mysterious plot unfolds before them. Trying to discover the power behind the attempt on Devon's life. The six friends start to make connections to a powerful company and a dangerous supernatural organization. While searching for answers they are put in the path of dangerous enemies, powerful magics and a sinister leader who's behind it all